W9-CNX-730

Sweet Dreams, My Little One

A Treasury of Stories for Bedtime

SANDY CREEK

New York

Can't you sleep, Dotty?

Tim Warnes

Tick-Tock!
Tick-Tock!

10

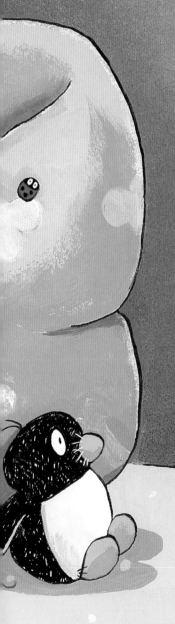

Dotty couldn't sleep.
It was her first night
in her new home.

She tried sleeping
upside down.

She tried
snuggling up
to Penguin.

She even tried
lying on the
floor.

AWOOOOOOOOOoooo

But still Dotty
couldn't sleep.

Dotty's howling woke up Pip the Mouse. "Can't you sleep, Dotty?" he asked. "Perhaps you should try counting the stars like I do."

But Dotty could
only count up to
one. *That* wasn't
enough to send
her to sleep.

What could she do next?

AWOoooooooooo

Susie the Bird was awake now. "Can't you sleep, Dotty?" she chirped. "I always have a little drink before I go to bed."

Chirp!

Chirp!

Dotty went to her bowl and
had a little drink.

Slurp!
Slurp!

But then she made
a tiny puddle.
Well *that*
wouldn't help!
What *could* Dotty
do to get to sleep?

AWOOOOoooooooo

Whiskers the Rabbit had woken up, too.
"Can't you sleep, Dotty?" he mumbled
sleepily. "I hide in my den at bedtime.
That always works."

23

Dotty dived under her blanket so that only her bottom was showing. But it was very dark under there with no light at all.

Dotty was too scared to go to sleep.

Flump!

Tommy the Tortoise poked his head from out of his shell.

"Can't you sleep, Dotty?" he sighed. "I like to sleep where it's bright and sunny."

Plod
Plod

Dotty liked the idea . . .

and turned on her flashlight!

"Turn it off, Dotty!"
shouted all her friends.
"*We* can't get to sleep now!"

Yikes!

Poor Dotty was too
tired to try anything else.
Then Tommy had a great idea!

He helped Dotty into her bed.
What Dotty needed for the first
night in her new home was . . .

to snuggle among *all*
her new friends. Soon
they were all fast asleep.
Good night, Dotty.

33

Little Bunny's Bathtime!

Jane Johnson

pictures by

Gaby Hansen

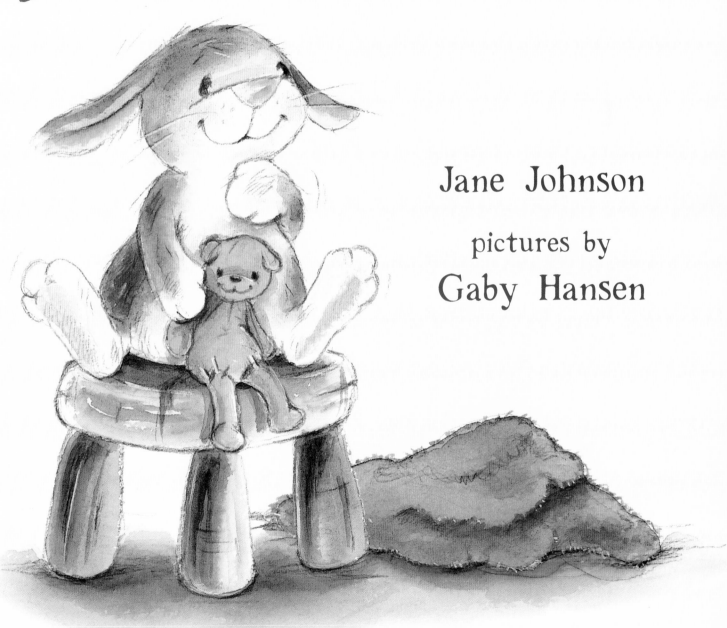

"Bathtime for my little rabbits!"
called Mrs. Rabbit, and her
children came running.
All except her youngest
little one.

"I don't want a bath,"
said Little Bunny.
"I want to keep playing."

"You really want to play all by
yourself?" asked Mrs. Rabbit.
Little Bunny nodded, but
now he wasn't so sure.

"Well, you be good while
I'm busy with the others,"
said Mrs. Rabbit, plopping
her bunnies into the bathtub.

"Swish, splish, splash,"
sang the little rabbits happily,
swirling their bubbles around.
Little Bunny wanted
to play, too.

"Look at me!" he called,
hiding behind the towels.

"Yes, dear," said Mrs. Rabbit, but
she went on washing the others.
"Tickly, wiggly, giggly toes," sang
the little rabbits as they wiggled their
feet in the water.

"Guess where I am?"
shouted Little Bunny,
hidden in the
laundry basket.

"Found you," smiled his
mother, lifting the lid.

But she turned back
to finish washing
the others.

"Out you go," puffed Mrs. Rabbit,
lifting her children out of the tub.

"Rub-a-dub-dub, you've all had a scrub," she laughed. "What lovely, clean bunnies you are!"

Little Bunny was upset.
He wanted his mommy
to notice him.

So he
climbed
up . . .

and up . . .

as far as he could.

But suddenly . . .

SPLASH!

He fell into the bathtub!

"Oh my!" cried Mrs. Rabbit, scooping
him out of the water right away.
Little Bunny gazed up at her happily.
"I'm ready for my bath now, Mommy,"
he said, smiling sweetly.

Mrs. Rabbit couldn't
help smiling back.
  "Off you go to play
quietly," she said to
her other rabbits.

Then she ran
fresh water and gave
Little Bunny his
own special bath.

"Soapy ears and soapy toes, and soapy little
bunny nose!" sang Mrs. Rabbit.
She washed his ears while he played
with the new bubbles.
"I love you, Mommy," said Little Bunny.
"I love you too, sweetheart!"

She washed his back while
he played with his boat.
  "You're the best mommy in the
whole world," said Little Bunny.
  "And you're my precious
little bunnykin."

She dried his fur
and whiskers, and said,
"Mmm, you smell
so nice and clean!"

And Little Bunny kissed his mommy
and hugged her tight.

"There now, all done," sighed Mrs. Rabbit.
"It's time for bed. Where are my other
little rabbits?"

She found them in the kitchen.
"Oh no! What a mess!" cried
Mrs. Rabbit. "You're all dirty again.
You all need another bath!"

"Yes," giggled Little Bunny.
"All except me!"

Time to Sleep, Alfie Bear!

Catherine Walters

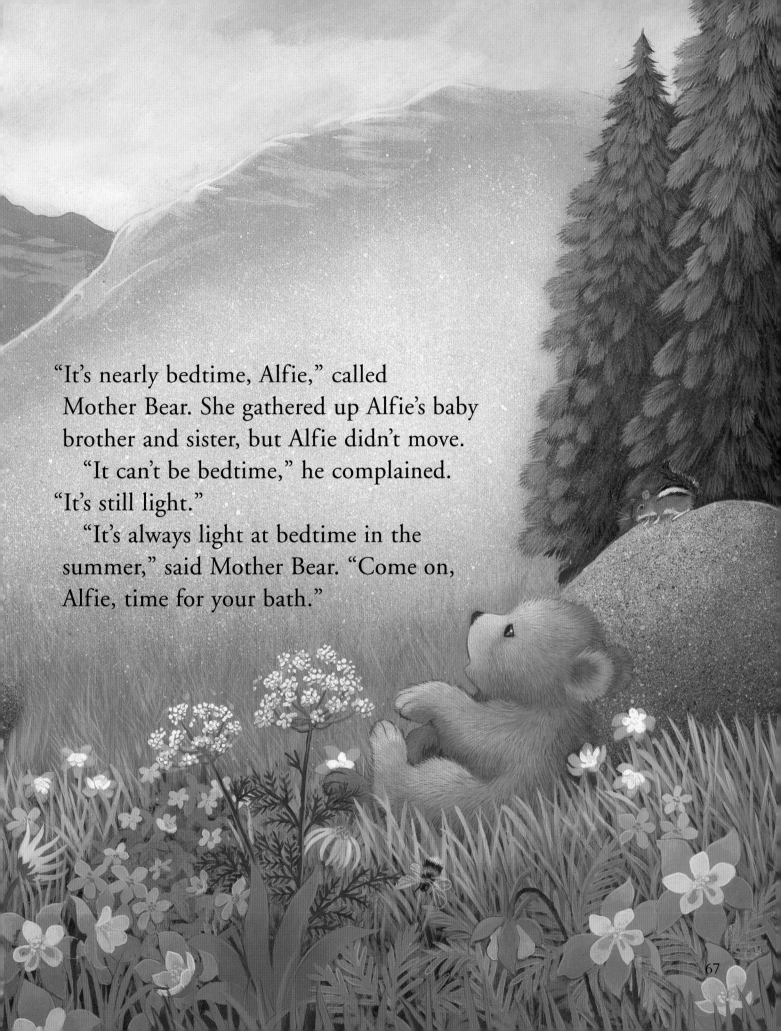

"It's nearly bedtime, Alfie," called
Mother Bear. She gathered up Alfie's baby
brother and sister, but Alfie didn't move.
    "It can't be bedtime," he complained.
"It's still light."
    "It's always light at bedtime in the
summer," said Mother Bear. "Come on,
Alfie, time for your bath."

Mother Bear took Alfie and
the babies to the lake.

"We'll all have a nice relaxing bath
to make us sleepy," said Mother Bear.

Alfie sat by the water's edge. It was
still warm after a long sunny day and
the fish were jumping to catch the
evening flies.

"Huh! The fish aren't going to bed,"
thought Alfie. "Why should I?"

It gave him an idea . . .

"Look, Mother Bear," shouted Alfie.
"I don't have to go to bed! I'm a fish!"

He began to jump and dive and splash.
The babies loved it. They laughed and
splashed too.
   "Don't do that," sighed Mother Bear.
"The babies are getting too excited.
They'll never go to sleep."

When they all calmed down,
Mother Bear took them back to
the cave.

"It's a warm night," she said.
"Go and get some nice, cool
grass for bedding, Alfie. That
will help you sleep."

Alfie went outside and pulled
up a few pawfuls of grass.

Over in the meadow, some owls were
swooping, ready for their evening hunt.
  "The owls aren't going to bed,"
thought Alfie. "Why should I?"

Alfie rushed back into the cave and began to flap his arms. Grass flew everywhere.

"Look! I'm an owl!" he hooted. "I don't need to go to bed. I'm just getting up!"

"Oh Alfie, stop that!" groaned Mother Bear. "Look, the babies are throwing all their lovely bedding around, too. None of you will have anywhere to sleep."

At last, Alfie and the babies were safely
in bed but still they didn't go to sleep.

"I think you need a nice, gentle song,"
said Mother Bear. "Now, close your eyes."

Alfie wasn't listening. Outside, he
could hear wolves howling.

"The wolves aren't going to sleep,"
he thought. "Why should I?"

"Look, I'm a wolf! HOOOOWL!" said Alfie.

"OW, OW, OW!" shrieked the babies, kicking their feet.

Mother Bear wasn't pleased. "That's enough, Alfie," she growled. "I don't want any little wolves in the cave. You can wait outside until the babies are asleep."

"Hooray!" cried Alfie, running outside.
    The sun had set and the air was full
of dust and shadows. Alfie charged
across the meadow, tipped back his
head, and howled again,
"HOOOOWL!"
    Then, from somewhere close by,
someone answered him,
    "HOOOOWL!"

Alfie jumped. There in front of him was
a wolf cub, with his family close by.

The cub sniffed him all over.

"Are you a wolf?" it asked. "You sound
like one, but you don't look like one."

"All little wolf cubs should be in bed
by now," growled Mother Wolf.

"Are you sure you're a wolf?" called
a big, gruff voice . . .

". . . because you look like a little bear to me!"
It was Father Bear, coming to take
him home.
"I'm a bear, I'm a bear!" shouted Alfie.
The big wolves turned and walked away.
"Goodnight, little bear," called the
wolf cub, following them into the trees.

Father Bear snuggled Alfie into his fur.

"So you're a bear?" he said. "But are you a sleepy bear all ready for bed?"

Night had fallen, and the sky sparkled with stars.

"No," said Alfie. "I'm not–"

But before he could finish speaking, he had fallen fast asleep.

Two Hungry Bears

Linda Cornwell and Jane Chapman

Big Brown Bear and
Little Bear shared a
cozy cave. They shared
each other's company . . .

94

and they shared
each other's food.
Little Bear nibbled
around the edges . . .

and Big Brown Bear
munched up the middles.
In this way, they got
along very well.

But one bright autumn day,
Little Bear woke up
feeling EXTRA hungry
and Big Brown Bear
woke up feeling
MONSTROUSLY
hungry!
"I'll buy some food
for both of us," said
Little Bear.
"That's very kind
of you, Little Bear,"
answered Big Brown
Bear sleepily, and
he crept right
back to bed.

Little Bear went out shopping and bought some things to take back to Big Brown Bear. But she found she was so hungry . . .

that she ate everything
straight away—
pies and pastries,
peanuts and puddings,

chocolates and cheeses,
crisps and cakes—

from sides to middles,
middles to sides
AND BACK AGAIN!

Meanwhile, Big Brown Bear's tummy was
RRRRUMMMBLING very loudly—so loudly
that the walls of the cave began to shake.
"I've been thinking," said Big Brown Bear,
"maybe *I* should be out shopping for Little Bear."
So off he went with his big bag . . .

but when he had filled
it right up, he found
he was so hungry,
he could not wait.

He began by
munching just
the middles.

But then he set to work on sausages,
strawberries and sandwiches,
not to mention tangerines,
caramel apples and peach pies . . .

AND hamburgers, custard and fries . . .

AND biscuits, spaghetti and soup . . .

AND
pizzas, salads and
ice-cream . . .

AND
tomatoes,
jello and
corn on the cob—
and one small
grape.

107

Big Brown Bear ate tops, bottoms,
sides, and middles.
There was just no stopping him!

But when he had finished eating,
he began to feel very, very full
and very, very guilty.
He had nothing left for Little Bear.

Big Brown Bear staggered back home where
Little Bear was waiting patiently for him.
"Did you find any nice middles to munch?"
Little Bear asked him. *I can see that you did!*
she thought to herself.
Big Brown Bear could only nod his head.

"Did you come across any tasty edges to nibble?"
asked Big Brown Bear. *It certainly looks as
though you might have!* he thought to himself.

They sat
down together—
very carefully.
"I saved you half
of a cracker,"
said Big Brown Bear.
"It still has four
edges to nibble."
"I saved you three
quarters of a banana,"
said Little Bear.
"It's all middle—
no edges
at all!"

113

After a while, Big
Brown Bear yawned.
"I think I'll skip supper,"
he said. "I'm feeling
a little too tired."
"An early night will
do us both good,"
agreed Little Bear.
They spent an awfully
long time brushing
their teeth . . .

before Big Brown Bear snuggled into his
bed, and Little Bear crept quietly into hers.
"Let's buy the food together tomorrow,"
said Big Brown Bear with a yawn.
But tomorrow was a long, long time away
because . . .

Big Brown Bear and
Little Bear slept, with
their tummies pleasantly full,
all through the winter until
SPRING!

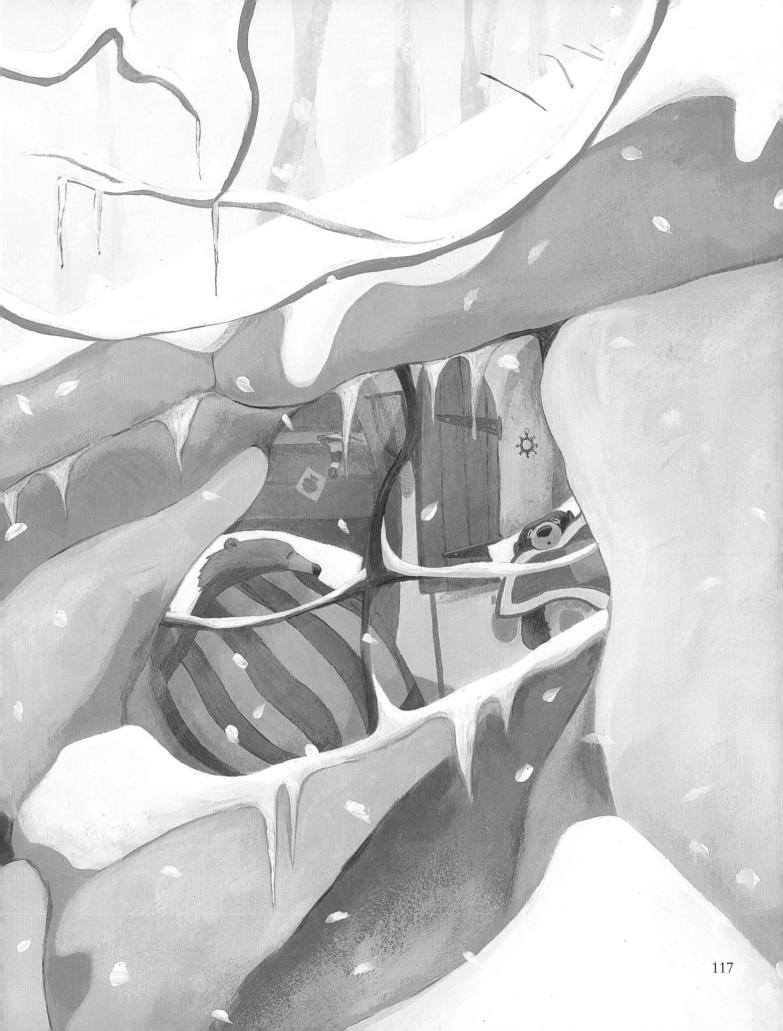